I0729744

Book design by Peter Nowell

Titles in Francesco by Franck Jalleau

Text in Capita by Dieter Hofrichter

Ensorcelled

Eliot Peper

Also by Eliot Peper

Foundry

Reap3r

Veil

Breach

Borderless

Bandwidth

True Blue

Neon Fever Dream

Cumulus

Exit Strategy

Power Play

Version 1.0

Sometimes a story is the only thing that can save your life.

1

How do you make a game?

A simple question with a not-so-simple answer.

Sweet child, I hope you will forgive an old man his rambling, because that's the risk you run asking someone so close to the end about the beginning.

2

THERE IS MAGIC in this world. There are spells. There are potions. There are dragons. And there are tricks too, things that only pretend to be magic. It is not always easy to tell the difference. It takes art. It takes skill. It takes a lifetime, at least.

I will tell you a story about finding that magic. This is no tale for the selfish or the faint of heart. Magic offers you everything, but it asks everything of you in return.

So if you're not willing to bare your heart and stake your soul, better to set this book aside and return to your life untroubled. You have my blessing. But if you're one of those rare few who can't help but go where the trouble is, then I welcome your company.

Together, we will get into trouble. We will seek the magic and endure the tricks. I don't know if we'll survive the journey, but the only voyages worth embarking on are those that venture into the unknown.

3

IT ALL STARTED the day before *Ark of the Shadow Moon* launched.

Every Clandestine Studios game is a labyrinthine masterpiece. As the galaxy's most notorious thief, you sneak through gorgeously realized worlds in pursuit of jealously protected treasures, evading guards, outsmarting security systems, and breaking hearts along the way. I had invested hundreds of hours into *The Singularity Amulet* and could recite the answers to the robot sphinx's paradoxical riddles in *Quinten's Kernel* from memory.

The games adapt to who you are, the characters, story, levels, and lore evolving in real-time to complement your history, worldview, and behavior, the experience personalized to maximize the sense of meaning you derive from it. Each session maintains the perfect balance of challenge and accomplishment. Each new release from Clandestine Studios is a significant cultural event.

I had been scouring the forums for clues that might indicate something—anything!—about *Ark of the Shadow Moon*. Concept art. Feature lists. Mechanics. Or the holy grail: actual gameplay clips. There was nothing but swirling rumor. True to its name, Clandestine Studios was famously tightlipped about anything in development, and the only verifiable facts about *Ark of the Shadow Moon* were the title and the release date. So I drew intricately detailed scenes of what I imagined the game would be like, and waited.

Tomorrow.

Tomorrow, my prayers would be answered.

Tomorrow, my world would change.

Tomorrow—

And that was the moment Dad entered my room (without knocking) to ask whether I was packed.

4

Packed for what?

No. I did not remember the camping trip my parents and their old college friends had been planning for months. I had far more important things on my mind.

No. I hadn't been listening when they mentioned it over dinner last night. With the impending *Ark of the Shadow Moon* release, I had grown accustomed to tuning out small talk in favor of imagining what it would be like to play for the first time.

No. I hadn't noticed them prepping gear. My parents are always rearranging the apartment for no apparent reason. It seems to be a common hobby among adults. Personally, I don't see the appeal, but I'm happy for them, really I am.

Let's be reasonable. I respect that you're excited about getting dirty, eating bad food, and sleeping on the ground, but they're your friends, not mine, and *Ark of the Shadow Moon* comes out tomorrow, so why don't you go on your trip, and I'll stay right here. Both of us get what we want. Win-win.

Yes, I know your friends have kids too, but I don't know them. They're not *my* friends. Would *you* be excited about going on a camping trip with a bunch of complete strangers? I don't think so.

Sure, in theory it can be nice to meet new people, but in practice it's usually just awkward, and you know what's not a theory but a cold, hard fact? *Ark of the Shadow Moon*'s release date, which is tomorrow. Did I mention that yet? Tomorrow. Yes, tomorrow. So, how about that win-win?

But Dad was not interested in a win-win. He was not interested in a tantrum either. He was even less interested in my final, desperate appeal to Mom, which turned out to be a nonstarter. The only thing my parents were interested in was crushing my dream like an olive in the mill of "because I said so."

And that's how I ended up spending what should have been an evening replete with sweet anticipation throwing a sweatshirt and a flashlight and a sketchbook into my backpack and cursing the irony of a species having worked so hard to get out of the jungle choosing to return to it for so-called pleasure.

5

WE LEFT the next morning before the sun came up.

I sat in the back seat and pressed my face against the window, my breath steaming up the glass. The streets were empty. The shops were closed. Towers loomed on either side. Streetlights whipped by, their stark illumination making the surrounding darkness yet darker. It was as if we were sneaking out of San Francisco, making our escape before the other residents woke up and noticed our absence.

Can you be kidnapped by your own parents? That's what this was: non-consensual camping.

The car slowed as we approached a stop sign and I imagined opening the door and leaping out. I would fling my grappling hook onto the neon facade of Dumpling Empire, run up the wall, pull myself onto the roof, dodge past the hissing chimneys and, using their steam as cover, jump across the narrow alley and catch myself on the metal frames that extended just farther than the windows of the adjacent skyscraper, move hand-over-hand around the corner of the building, flip back to catch the arched limb of the bay tree in the pocket park, shimmy down, and sprint back through dark streets toward home, arriving just in time for launch. It would be epic.

But then we accelerated away from the stop sign and I was still sitting in the back, fingering the seatbelt.

There's a turn you have to make to get from our apartment to the freeway where, if you know what you're looking for, you can catch a glimpse of Clandestine Studios through a gap between a loading dock and a community garden. I craned my neck, and yes, there it was. Warm light glowed from the windows in the red brick wall. I imagined the people inside preparing for the big day. Running on fumes and clinically inadvisable amounts of coffee. Giving each other high fives. Running down final checklists. Making sure everything was ready for players from around the world to mob *Ark of the Shadow Moon.*

I sighed as the center of my universe disappeared behind us.

We ascended the ramp onto the Bay Bridge. Buildings zipped past and, feeling like a voyeur, I witnessed brief moments of strangers' morning routines through their apartment windows. A woman doing pull-ups. A family eating breakfast in a galley kitchen.

An old man trimming a bonsai. I imagined how I would draw each window-framed scene and envied each and every subject their freedom.

Ahead, the sun breached the Oakland hills, momentarily blinding me.

Behind, the city receded, a glass and steel jewel bathed in dawn's red-gold, flaws rectified by distance.

6

I FELL INTO that special kind of road-trip stupor. The sound of the highway, the rocking of the car, the world whizzing by at tremendous speed even though it feels like you're making no headway whatsoever.

I didn't say a word to my parents. If they insisted on tearing me away from *Ark of the Shadow Moon*, the least they could do was let me brood in peace.

My brooding must have slipped into dozing, because the next thing I knew Dad was shaking my shoulder.

I rubbed my eyes. We were on a dirt road cut into the side of a cliff. To the right, a sheer granite wall. To the left, a narrow valley hundreds of feet below. No cars. No houses. No people. Just peak after peak in all directions and a single track winding ever higher into the jagged mountains.

Unfastening my seatbelt, I slid out of the car and stretched stiff muscles, yawning. Ahead, the road took a hairpin switchback to approach the cliff's summit, but erosion had cut deep channels into the dirt, and rocks jutted out at odd angles. The road's condition was worst at the tightest point of the turn, a mess of chunky stone and loose gravel. Unless you were driving a tank, it was impassable.

"Come on," said Dad, and we walked up around the turn together, stopping every few feet to assess the situation from multiple angles.

"How would you do it?" he asked, which took me off guard.

Raising a hand to shade my eyes, I looked up to the heat-rippled haze on the horizon and said, "I'd turn around and go home."

But he just stood there quietly, letting silence negotiate on his behalf.

In *Quinten's Kernel*, you have to escape the cave system in a motorbike with the rescued biohacker riding sidecar. Pursued by thousands of bats genetically modified to carry box-jellyfish venom, you race through caverns, dodge stalagmites, duck stalactites, and jump bottomless fissures in a desperate attempt to reach the surface before running out of fuel.

I died seventeen times trying to beat that level.

Cocking my head to the side, I imagined how I'd take the turn in the motorbike. Then I squatted and began pushing rocks up against an exposed root. The sun beat down. Dad knelt to help. The hot air filled with dust and pine resin. I found a fallen branch and we used it to lever a boulder off to the side. Sweat trickled down my back. We kicked gravel into holes and piled loose stones to build ramps up deep ruts.

Finally, it was done.

I walked the line.

My parents watched.

Then Mom took the wheel and Dad spotted from behind. I ran ahead, giving pointers. Mom bounced over broken rocks, took the high line on the left around the deepest rut, angled the wheels to ascend the ramp to the first boulder, popped up on the root—it was working!—but suddenly the wheels spun free, kicking up gravel.

My heart leapt into my throat and a vision descended over me: the car sliding backward, picking up speed, slamming into Dad, and going off the edge of the cliff, smashing a spur of rock on the way down, flipping end over end until it exploded on impact with the valley floor hundreds of feet below. With my parents dead and our vehicle destroyed, I'd have to hike all the way back down this lonely road until I stumbled onto the highway—a self-made orphan.

"Stop," called Dad, and Mom engaged the emergency brake.

Dad waved me over and I found I could breathe again, move again. He showed me how to wedge larger stones behind each tire. Then we stepped back. Mom edged forward and the tires held.

A shiver ran through me despite the heat. There were no save points here, no second chances, let alone seventeenth chances.

7

BEYOND THE CLIFF was a forest. Beyond the forest was a ridge. Beyond the ridge was another ridge. Beyond that ridge was yet another ridge. And when we finally reached the top of the third ridge, a new world opened up in front of us.

A turquoise lake lay nestled in a ring of snow-capped peaks. Pine and chaparral covered the lower slopes. A graceful waterfall churned up spray at the far shore. And in the middle of the lake was an island. The setting sun bathed the scene in honeyed light, enriching every color, highlighting every texture, lengthening every shadow, transforming the landscape into something sacred, something secret—an infinite library of hiding places and forking paths and little nooks and rugged vantages. I had never seen anything like it.

"What *is* this place?" I asked.

Mom pointed at the island. "That's where we're headed."

As we drove down the winding track to the shore, I looked at the back of my parents' bobbing heads and smiled, though I was careful not to let them see it. This might not be *Ark of the Shadow Moon*, but maybe there were treasures here worth hunting after all.

8

THE CANOE CRUNCHED up onto the gravel beach. Mom vaulted over the side to secure it, and then we hauled it up above the water line and began to unload gear.

Tall pines lined the island's cove. A few kayaks and paddle boards lay on the grass next to our canoe. Noise filtered down a path through the trees. Voices. Laughter. Violin. Birds darted down to snatch bugs hovering near the surface of the water.

My parents each picked up one side of the cooler and began lugging it up the path. I put on my backpack, picked up a dry-bag in each hand, and followed. Before stepping into the shadows beneath the pines, I threw one last glance over my shoulder.

Across the water, high on the mountain ridge opposite the cove, a single tree stood alone against the darkling sky, catching the last of the dying light. I'd never before have described a plant as charismatic, but there was something special about that tree, something that lodged inside you like a dream, or a hook.

9

CAMP LAY IN THE wind-shadow of the rocky peak at the center of the island. A large bug tent had been pitched over a picnic table. Shade sails were ratcheted to surrounding trees. A fire danced in a stone-lined pit, throwing off sparks. Fairy lights were strung everywhere, colors shifting and pulsing so slowly that you might not notice if you didn't stare.

People were sitting around the fire eating and drinking and talking animatedly. A golden retriever chased a sheepdog in tight circles. A woman stood on an ancient stump playing the violin, body swaying with the haunting, rhythmic music, fingers dancing up and down the neck faster than I could follow in the flickering orange light.

There was a perfect moment where we took it all in without anyone noticing our presence.

Then the dogs scented us and began to bark and the woman leapt from the stump and the people rushed over and there were hugs and slaps on the back and introductions and jokes and offers to help with the gear and the tent and enjoinders to eat and myriad beverages offered and the happy chaos engulfed our family.

It was a lot.

It was also when I met Lenny and Theo for the first time.

They were the only other kids on the trip. Theo was tall and athletic with an open face and laughing eyes and the kind of inborn confidence that makes you wonder whether he had ever experienced self-doubt, even as a novelty. Lenny was agile and serious with dirt streaked across her pale cheek and a gaze that was intense to the point of feral. They were eager to return to an all-consuming game that our arrival had interrupted, and when I declined Theo's invitation to join in, they rushed off.

At the time, I had no idea that we would fall so completely into each other's orbits. I couldn't predict the future. And even if I had, what could I have done differently?

Well, if I'm honest, there's a lot I could have done differently, but I'm getting ahead of myself. The evening we arrived at camp, I was overwhelmed by these strange people and this strange place and seeing something in my parents shift as they greeted their old friends and the intimidating intimacy of Lenny and Theo's dynamic and the familiar feeling of wanting desperately to belong, but knowing deep down that I didn't.

10

THEO infuriated me.

He was one of those people who are just amazing at everything. When he threw a frisbee, it drew a clean arc straight to its target. Everyone laughed at his jokes. The light always hit him at a photogenic angle. He was a great listener. He assumed good intent. His smile was infectious and his evident affection for Lenny was heartfelt. He was obviously going to be valedictorian and probably president. Theo navigated the physical world with the same competence with which my thief navigated the digital. The natural ease of his bearing made me feel like an alien arriving on Earth for the first time who didn't know what to say or how to act, and this sense of insecurity left me sullen and standoffish.

Of course, Theo was nothing but kind to me, and the injustice of my resentment only made me resent him all the more. Not only did I envy him, but I blamed him for my jealousy, and despised myself for doing so. The unfairness of his general excellence compounded the unfairness of being dragged on this dumb trip in the first place.

Whenever it got to be too much, I'd grab my sketchbook and stalk off into the woods.

11

WHEN I'M NOT STEALING fusion reactor designs from the mad scientist's submarine lab, I'm drawing. I love drawing because it makes you look at things differently.

Say you want to sketch a portrait of your aunt. Needing to commit pencil to paper forces you to notice all kinds of details you'd normally gloss over. How her hair is starting to come in gray at the roots. The left dimple that forms in her cheek when she offers one of her signature half-smiles. How light falls across her neck. The complex astrological signs formed by freckles that never quite fade, even in winter.

The world contains a surprising amount of detail. And it's not just the world. The same is true of your imagination.

Say you want to draw the surreal dream you woke up from this morning, the one where you were floating through a cloud city. What perspective should you take? Were the columns Ionic or Corinthian? Was the city *made* of cloud, or was it built from conventional materials but sitting *on* a cloud? Could the many interlocking stairways support weight, or did residents float around as you had? Memory lets the dream hide in a general emotional impression, but drawing it means you have to commit to specific creative decisions. Drawing is an engine for asking questions, for delving deeper.

Noticing is just the first step. When you draw, you can't just ask questions, you have to answer them. You have to move the pencil over the paper such that the resulting mark will suggest your aunt's dimple. You have to hash in texture along the transition between fluffy cumulus underside and the built environment of your sky-borne metropolis.

To draw is not to record an image, whether you're appraising it with your physical or your mind's eye. To draw is to lay out a series of clues that will summon an image of your aunt or your cloud city in someone else's mind.

That's why Picasso could draw a flamingo with a single unbroken line. The line does not resemble a flamingo, it represents it in a way anyone looking at the drawing can intuitively decode. Drawing is a two-part transformation: distilling an image from one mind into symbols that can be reassembled by another.

Drawing is all of these things and more. And for me, drawing was also something else: an escape. I loved drawing because it made me look at things differently, and I loved drawing because it made me forget that people might be looking at me.

12

"WHAT ARE YOU DRAWING?"

I slammed my sketchbook shut.

"Nothing," I said.

It was Lenny. I had snuck away from camp to my favorite rock on the island's shore. This place was my refuge, and now Lenny had violated it.

"You can't draw nothing," she said. "There's nothing to draw."

I flushed, and then held back a defensive rejoinder. From anyone else, her comment would have come off as passive-aggressive, but she said it as a straightforward statement of fact, which made me feel silly, which, in turn, made me frustrated enough to try honesty.

"I don't want to show you what I'm drawing," I said.

"Oh." She blinked. "Well, why didn't you just say that then?"

"I..." I said, floundering. "Since when do people say what they mean?"

She nodded seriously. "It's very confusing," she said. "I used to think words were for saying what you're thinking, but now I'm not so sure."

I didn't know what to say to that, so I just sat there, which felt awkward to me, but apparently didn't bother her, because she sat down next to me on the sun-baked stone.

Ripples lapped at the base of the boulder. Lenny wore what she always wore: a purple one-piece bathing suit. Her hair was tangled. Her feet were bare. There was a splotch of sunscreen on her forehead that hadn't been rubbed in properly.

"Where's Theo?" I asked. I assumed she'd only have sought me out if her best friend was unavailable. I'd spent the past two days trying to avoid them, despite my parents' embarrassingly blatant attempts to foment friendship.

"Dunno," she said.

The surface of the lake spread out before us, a vast mirror reflecting the mountains rising up from the far shore. It would be so cool to use that mirror as a screen. I could scramble up the face of the ridge, find a good lookout spot, and boot up *Ark of the Shadow Moon* on the largest display on the planet. Wind swell would distort parts of the image, the island would occlude some of it, and fish would breach it every so often, but those imperfections would accentuate the other-worldliness of gazing through a portal into elsewhere.

"Where are you?" asked Lenny.

Startled, I said, "Here."

She snorted.

"What?" I demanded.

"Come on," she said, pushing herself up. "I want to show you something."

13

Lenny led me farther around the island. The way she moved reminded me of the nameless thief you play in the Clandestine Studios games. Her bare feet made no sound, while I kept stepping on fallen branches and dry leaves. She didn't look like she was trying to go fast, but I struggled to keep up, prickly manzanita pulling at my shirt and scratching my arms. There was no path, but she didn't hesitate, taking a route that twisted and turned and traversed a sandstone cliff to reach a slender crescent beach.

Without even pausing for breath, Lenny waded into the sparkling water and dove in as soon as she was deep enough. After a few powerful dolphin kicks, she came up for air, shook out her hair, and looked back at me.

"What are you waiting for?" she asked. "Let's go."

I shifted uncomfortably. "Isn't it cold?" I asked, stalling.

"Only for a minute," she said. "You get used to it."

Who knew how deep the lake was, or what lived in its depths? The sliver of bottom I could see through the shallow water by the shore looked muddy. I didn't want to take off my t-shirt. Plus, I didn't have any sunscreen on under it. And what was I supposed to do afterward, pull on dry socks over wet dirty feet? No thank you.

"I'll just watch from here," I said hopefully.

"Come *on*," said Lenny with a glare that could melt titanium.

So I turned away self-consciously, dropped my backpack, and stripped off my t-shirt, draping it over a bush. I removed my shoes and socks and double knotted my board shorts' drawstring so they wouldn't accidentally slip off. With no more credible excuses for dawdling, I picked my way down to the water and dipped a toe in.

"It's freezing!" I said.

"I told you," she said. "You get used to it. The faster you get in, the faster you adjust."

I wasn't about to trust the advice of an obvious psychopath, so I eased my way in inch by frigid inch while Lenny treaded water and rolled her eyes. Mud squished between my toes. I inhaled sharply as the water reached my groin. Looking down, I saw my nipples stiffen, which made me blush.

As soon as I was chest-deep, Lenny struck out, following the curving shore. She swam like a seal, lithe and effortless. I rushed to follow, conscious of all the energy wasted by my lunging, splashy strokes.

We passed the end of the crescent beach, and now cliffs rose sheer from water which had turned a deeper shade of cobalt as the bottom receded below us. Just as I was about to suggest we turn around, Lenny dove beneath the surface, kicking down.

I waited, treading water. How long had it been? Was she still holding her breath? I didn't think I could hold my breath that long. Seconds ticked by and my nerves frayed. Could she have gotten stuck? Should I go after her? If I went to get help, we wouldn't return in time if she was drowning.

Then Lenny surged up in a halo of bubbles.

"Over here," she said excitedly.

She handed me her goggles, which I hadn't even noticed she'd been wearing. I fumbled with them, adjusting the strap until they fit snugly over my eyes.

"Hurry," she said. "I don't know how long she'll stay."

"Who's 'she'?" I asked, not liking the sound of that.

"See for yourself," she said.

14

So, against my better judgement, I sucked in a deep breath, ducked my head under water, and swam into hazy darkness. The bottom was obscured by silt, but the cliff extended below the surface, the sandstone dappled by sunbeams that penetrated the shallows. Tiny fish schooled through the refracted light, flowing together, apart, and together again. Their movement was simultaneously coordinated and random, as if directed by an unseen, over-caffeinated choreographer.

I came up for air. "The fish are cool," I said. "It's like they're dancing."

"Uh huh," she said. "What else did you see?"

"Umm," I said. "I couldn't really see the

bottom very well, but the cliff looks neat underwater."

"Look under the shelf," she said.

I dove again and kicked forward toward the cliff, which did form a sort of underwater shelf before dropping away into shadow. I swam closer, scanning left and right, looking for anything unusual. Nothing. Just water and striated rock and—

—a flash of movement—

—cold adrenaline flooded through me. I thrashed back as my stomach clenched and my heart hammered against my ribs. Panic overwhelmed my mind with static.

I came up gasping and yelled, "Snake!"

We had to get out of here. We had to get back to the beach. Lenny was a fast swimmer. That meant I'd be struggling in her wake, an easy target. Predators were attracted to any form of weakness.

"Yes!" said Lenny, green eyes bright. "Isn't she beautiful?"

"It's a *snake*," I said, suddenly conscious that I was marooned in the wilderness with a serpent and a madwoman. "Lenny, we have to get to safety. Let's *go*."

"Safety?" Lenny frowned. "She won't bite us."

"How could you possibly know that?" I demanded.

"Garter snakes aren't venomous," she said as if this were the most obvious thing in the world.

"So you thought it would be a good idea to surprise me with a snake?" I asked, my voice shuttling between sarcasm and disbelief.

"Exactly," she said, pleased. "I love how the lateral stripes set off the mottled olive color. Ooo, and the dorsal scales are keeled. But my favorite part is how she swims. I wish I could swim like that."

Lenny's sincerity doused my fear-fueled anger. Apparently no amount of irony could penetrate her earnestness. So I took a deep breath, waited for my erratic heart-rate to settle, and ducked down to take another look.

The snake didn't so much swim as *flow* through the water, its slender body describing a never-ending series of wide, graceful curves. Despite Lenny's reassurances, instinctual terror fluttered in my chest, but I tamped it down, telling myself it would be ok, and, having done so, floated just beneath the surface, mesmerized.

Lenny was right.

The snake was beautiful.

15

THERE'S A LEVEL in *The Singularity Amulet* where you have to navigate a labyrinth carved into an asteroid to steal a cryptographic key lying on a chrome-plated plinth in its heavily shielded core. Armed guards float through the three-dimensional tunnel network, and blast doors hiss open and closed at random intervals to reconfigure the navigable route. You smuggle yourself into the asteroid in a shipping container supposedly carrying frozen burritos and wake up in the refrigeration unit. But six months of pharmaceutical-induced hibernation inside a carnitas-scented crate leaves you weak and nauseous, a shadow of your former self. Unable to fight the guards, you must carefully track their patrols, identifying hidden patterns in their movements that you can exploit to sneak to the center of the labyrinth and pocket the key undetected.

Just so, I attempted to decode our camp's morning rituals. The splatter and pop of eggs frying on a propane stove. The sacred rite of AeroPress coffee. The play of morning light on tousled hair. The tidying up of small things missed the night before. The dad jokes. The fresh fruit. The poppyseed bagels. The recitation of nonsense dreams. The dogs begging for treats. The arrival of late-risers. The slow build of conversation. The making of plans. The cycle of people disappearing to use the bathroom.

And then, finally, there it was: the gap in the pattern.

Shocked at my own boldness, I reached out, tapped Lenny's shoulder, led her behind the dense stand of aspens next to camp, and, before I could lose my nerve, thrust my sketchbook into her hands.

16

CLARK'S NUTCRACKERS ARE gray and black birds with sharp eyes and even sharper beaks.

They take their name from Captain William Clark who returned from his legendary expedition with a nutcracker specimen. Clark thought they were a kind of woodpecker because of their signature swoop, but he was wrong. They're actually in the crow family, so if you are lucky enough to see a flock of Clark's nutcrackers, then you have, in fact, witnessed a murder.

Rather than pecking wood, Clark's nutcrackers use that dagger beak to rip into whitebark pine cones and extract seeds that, weight for weight, contain more calories than chocolate. They store these delicious morsels in a special travel pouch beneath their tongues. During summer, an individual Clark's nutcracker will collect and bury ten thousand whitebark pine seeds. During winter, it will use its extraordinary spatial memory to dig up these buried treasures.

But memory, however extraordinary, is imperfect, and every so often, instead of being dug up and eaten, a seed will be forgotten and take root. Eventually, a little green shoot will poke up above the rocky subalpine soil, and, if it survives drought, flood, fire, relentless summer sun, punishing blizzards, hurricane-force winds, and voracious bunny rabbits, that shoot will grow into a sapling, which will grow into a whitebark pine tree, which will produce seeds of its own to offer the Clark's nutcrackers that perch on its upswept branches.

Eight hundred years before Clark and Meriwether Lewis set out on their exploratory mission, a member of the avian species that would one day bear his name buried a white-bark pine seed on the ridge above this lake and forgot all about it.

My sketchbook is full of drawings of that tree.

17

LENNY OPENED the sketchbook.

There was the tree on the ridge starkly profiled by the sun rising behind it. There was the tree front-lit by honeyed afternoon light that accentuated every texture and detail of the ridge's face. There was the tree as nothing but a splotch of darkness against the Milky Way.

But my drawings weren't limited to the landscape beneath our feet. There was the tree standing on the surface of *The Singularity Amulet*'s asteroid. There was the tree in the deepest, darkest cavern of *Quinten's Kernel*. There was the tree in what I imagined the opening scene of *Ark of the Shadow Moon* might be like. There was the tree in games that hadn't yet been made. And there was the tree reaching toward the sun from the roof of the

City's tallest skyscraper. There was the tree being trimmed by the elderly bonsai enthusiast whose apartment I'd glimpsed. There was the tree hopelessly enmeshed in endless variations of itself, branches twining into roots twining into yet more branches.

Lenny turned the pages slowly, often flipping back and forth between sketches. She traced heavy lines with her finger and used her nail to scratch the crosshatched shading. Desperate for a reaction, I couldn't tear my eyes from her face, but her expression remained solemn and unreadable.

"What do you think?" I asked when I couldn't stand it anymore.

She continued to stare at the drawings for so long I began to wonder if she hadn't heard me. But just as I opened my mouth to repeat the question, she closed the sketchbook, handed it back, and hit me with the full force of her laser gaze.

"After everyone goes to sleep"—she said—
"meet me at the shore."

18

I LAY IN MY SLEEPING BAG, as far from sleep as
it was possible to be. My mind raced and my
heart galloped alongside, trying to keep pace.
I curled and uncurled my toes in a vain
attempt to bleed off excess anxiety.

Through the darkness, I could just make
out the crossed poles holding up the arched
roof of our tent. Thinking ahead, I'd stashed
my jacket by the tent flap and left my shoes
right outside. I wore socks inside the sleeping
bag and my beanie was pulled down over my
ears.

Indistinct adult conversation filtered in from where they were still hanging out by the fire. Theo's mom's violin slalomed through a funky, fiddly jig. An owl hooted off in the distance and I imagined all the small forest animals seeking what shelter they could find from the round-faced killer sliding through the night on silent wings.

I had been distracted all day, responding to questions with little more than a "huh?" and defaulting to staring off into the middle distance—truant even by my own absent-minded standards. No matter what transpired or who tried to catch my attention, I could not tear myself away from the memory of that binding stare, the echo of those words that were half invitation, half command.

Meet me at the shore.

At long last, the adults dispersed. Outside the tent, my parents talked in hushed voices as they brushed their teeth and got ready for bed. Rolling onto my side, I closed my eyes and slowed my breathing. They unzipped the flap and clambered into the tent as quietly as they could, shimmying into their sleeping bags and wiggling around to get comfortable. Through it all, I pretended to sleep.

Eventually, all outside voices ceased as the other adults retired, and the only sounds were the creaking of the tent, the whisper of the trees, and my parents' breathing, which, from only a few feet away, seemed improbably loud. I followed the inhales and exhales, waiting for the rhythm to settle. Once Mom started twitching and Dad started snoring, I forced myself to count slowly to one hundred.

When the moment finally came, I couldn't move. My mind knew that it was time to go but my body was locked in place as if by some invisible magnet. I vibrated with tension and then, with a monumental act of will, extended one pinky finger. The magnetism melted away, and I could move again.

Inch by painstaking inch, I slid out of my sleeping bag and crawled to the tent flap. Mom's legs twitched as I reached over them to grab my jacket and I had to stifle a yelp. I froze and counted to ten, but my parents were still asleep. As slowly and smoothly as I could, I unzipped the flap, squeezed out through the corner with an awkward crab step, and zipped it back up again. I tied my shoes, stood up, and took a breath of the clean, cold night air.

The full moon painted camp in shades of silver, transforming the familiar space into a strange new world through which secrets and portents ran like occult electricity. Careful not to step on anything that might snap or crackle, I tiptoed through the picnic tables and past the doused fire that smelled of wet ash, half-expecting a golem to push up through the ring of still-hot stones like a dinosaur from an egg.

A dog barked, sharp in the stillness, and for a moment I thought all was lost, but then the bark trailed off into an uneven whine and

I realized it had not scented me, but was lost in a canine dream.

Maybe I was lost in a dream too.

Reaching the edge of camp, I peered into the darkness beneath the pines. So little moonlight filtered through their needles that I could barely make out the winding path. I looked back toward the tents, then forward again into the dark.

Meet me at the shore.

I took one step forward. Then another. And another. I stumbled. Caught myself. Pressed on. Shadows shifted and swirled around me. And then, before I knew it, I emerged onto the gravel beach.

"Get in," said Lenny matter-of-factly, indicating the front seat of the open-topped kayak she was nudging into the shallows. Unable to resist her down-to-Earth pragmatism amidst such an unearthly tableau, I stepped forward without question, but she grabbed the corner of my jacket and gave my feet a significant look.

Ah, yes, of course. Removing my socks and shoes, I waded in, and pulled myself aboard. She handed me a paddle, gave the craft a push, and vaulted lightly into the back as we slid out onto a quicksilver sea.

A voice in the back of my head, a voice that I normally lived my life by, said that this was a very bad idea indeed. I ignored it, and relished doing so.

19

THE LAKE WAS A MIRROR. The reflection of the moon, the stars, and the mountain was so perfect that it was hard to tell whether we were voyaging beneath or above them.

We cut across the pristine surface, our bow separating the heavens from their twin, leaving a V of darkness in our wake. I was awkward with the paddle at first, but Lenny coached me, and soon I was using my core instead of my arms and following through on every stroke. After a few false starts, we found a rhythm, and the kayak glided forward like a well-folded paper airplane thrown from a great height.

There was no chit-chat. No room for conversation. Only left, right, left, right, left, right. Only the feeling of surging ahead under your own power. Only the logic of the kayak which says embark! Explore!

My shoulders buzzed pleasantly. Hot spots kindled where my hands rubbed against the paddle. I am not one to heed the call of the wild. I let it go to voicemail while I attend to more important things like the call of *Ark of the Shadow Moon.*

There were no arks here. But there was a moon, and plenty of shadows. The night was alive. I was alive. For the moment at least, that was enough.

20

The waterfall roared.

Cold spray kissed our faces as Lenny steered us in to a mossy bank off to one side. With a nerve-racking amount of wobbling, we managed to disembark and then tied off the bowline so the kayak wouldn't float away.

Assuming we had reached our destination and grateful for a respite, I laid back on the springy moss to gaze up at the stars, but as soon as Lenny had double-knotted her shoes, she was up and moving again.

I scrambled to follow.

Under the moonlight, Lenny was a chrome-enameled elf weaving through trees and boulders, somehow finding a path where I couldn't see one. I stumbled along behind, desperate to keep her in view, convinced that if I lost her for a second, it would turn out to be forever.

We climbed up around the waterfall. The roar got so loud I couldn't hear my own footsteps and, where it was too steep to walk, the handholds were slick with spray. My lungs ached. My muscles burned. A stitch formed in my side. Under other circumstances, I would have been scared, but fear didn't have the opportunity to sink its claws into me because I only had time to do one thing: keep up.

Just when I thought I couldn't take it anymore, we came up over the ledge that formed the waterfall and the terrain leveled out a bit.

We were still ascending, but hiking, not climbing.

The river was a wide span of liquid silver where it approached the top of the falls. Lenny dipped her hands in the stream, and drank. I followed suit. As I felt the icy water flow through my fingers and looked back at where it fell away into empty air, I couldn't help but imagine being sucked over the edge by the current.

"Where are we going?" I asked.

Lenny glanced at me and frowned as if my question had been rhetorical, and, thus, annoying.

I hadn't known the answer when I asked the question, but her reaction made me realize that it had been obvious all along. I knew where we were going, and the thrill of that knowledge gave me goosebumps.

Thirst quenched, she was off again, and I with her.

We trekked for longer than seemed reasonable. From the island, this slope had looked like a steep, even face stretching from the lake to the ridge-line. But we hiked up and in, up and in, up and in, the landscape revealing itself in complex folds that were invisible to a distant observer.

Stone spires towered above us. The river pooled in smooth granite bowls and rushed over wide rocky fords. We pushed through prickly brush and vaulted rotting stumps, retracing our steps to find alternative routes when we reached impasses.

I thought we had reached just such an impasse when the mountain walls to either side closed in and the sound of tumbling water went from a murmur to a throaty growl.

Lenny stopped.

Catching my breath, I looked up to see that we were at the base of a steep canyon. The river tore through it, violent rapids churning around house-sized boulders.

Sitting down cross-legged on a patch of scratchy grass, Lenny produced two apples from her backpack, tossed me one, and bit into the other. I sat down next to her and took a bite. The fruit was crisp and sweet and made me realize how hungry I was. I wolfed it down.

"Why don't you like Theo?" asked Lenny.

"I like Theo," I said too quickly.

Pinching the stem, Lenny swung her apple core back and forth, eyes fixed on it.

"Tell me one thing about him," she said.

"He's... very good looking," I said, my voice betraying me by rising to make the statement sound like a question.

"Theo makes the best grilled cheese sandwiches on planet Earth," she said. "One of his chores is walking the dog, and if he sees that someone else didn't pick up after their dog, he does it for them. I've seen him come back from a walk with five bags of dog poop. Oh, and when he listens to music, he hears the melody, not the lyrics."

The silence swelled as the core swung back and forth, back and forth.

I started to say something, faltered, tried again. "I'm jealous of Theo," I said, staring at the pendulum and hoping my burning ears weren't visible in moonlight. What I was confessing to her, I was also admitting to myself for the first time. "You two know each other so well. I know it's dumb, but I... envy what you have. Your friendship."

Lenny grunted.

Then she tossed the core over her shoulder, stood up, and, once again, dug two objects out of her backpack and gave one to me.

"What's this?" I asked, squinting down.

"Headlamp," she said, donning hers. "Narrow gorge. Hard for light to get in."

21

THE GORGE WAS SO NARROW that I couldn't imagine finding a way up it. We just stood there for a moment, two tiny figures with cones of light shining from our foreheads facing a dark chasm of water and rock in frenzied melee.

I wanted to go back. I wanted to drink a steaming mug of hot chocolate and snuggle into my sleeping bag. I wanted to find a save point so we could respawn if something went wrong.

But when Lenny stepped forward, I did too.

Up close, the roaring darkness yielded to our headlamps. What had seemed a mono-lithic wall of impossibility transformed into a boulder here, a ledge there, and then sharply angled scree, and a log wedged into a deep crack. There was no way through. But there was always a next step. A next handhold. The gorge echoed and magnified the smash, crash, and boom of the rapids into a terrific din. My stomach tied itself into a single, solid knot. My heart established permanent residence in my throat. Fear banished thought. My blood ran hot and my sweat ran cold. There was no universe out there, no world beyond the gorge, nothing at all except for the crevice I could wedge three fingers into, the shelf along which we crawled.

And then: stars.

So many stars.

We emerged from the top of the gorge and the walls fell away and the Milky Way bloomed above us, a dazzling spill of glitter across black velvet. Clicking off our head-lamps, we proceeded by light that had spent countless eons traversing half the galaxy.

Fattened by tributaries below, here the river was a slender stream. We followed it up, up, up and, just under the ridge-line, arrived at

the source: a small pool encircled by a hemi-
sphere of solid rock as if the mountain held
it in cupped hands. The space was as quiet
and intimate as the gorge had been violent
and overwhelming. Lenny scrambled up one
side of the bowl and I the other so we both
reached the summit at the same time.

Then, slowly, hesitantly, I reached out and
touched the tree from my sketchbook. A strip
of dark, scaly bark spiraled up the smooth,
stout, bone-white trunk of naked wood that
twisted in wind-sculpted coils into branches
grasping at the nebulae hanging above us.
Roots fingered down to drink from the spring-
fed pool. Beyond the ridge where it stood
sentinel over our lake was mountain after
valley after mountain after valley, starlit
wilderness stretching out as far as we could
see. I had spent so many hours drawing this
tree, considering its form, admiring its domin-
ion, seeking to understand it through the act
of depicting it, and now it was real, it was here

in front of me and its sap was sticking to my fingers.

On the other side of the tree, Lenny was petting a bulging gnarl.

I leaned around the trunk to meet her eyes.

"Thank you for bringing me here," I said. "It's amazing you could remember the way at night."

"Remember?" she said, cocking her head to the side. "What do you mean?"

"You knew the path," I said. "Even in darkness."

"We found a path," she said.

"You've never been here before?" I asked, incredulous.

"First time," she said. "Just like you."

22

We sat on either side of the tree, feet dangling over the pool. In front of us, the valley lay open like a book and my eye traced the journey that had brought us from the island to the waterfall and up the winding canyon to this very spot.

"What do you think lives in the pool?" asked Lenny.

I looked down past our swinging feet. At the base of the empty scoop of rock, reflected stars glittered on the dark surface of the pool. It was a beautiful place. A holy place. But also so exposed to the elements, to extremity, to danger and pain and change. What sort of being might call this place home?

"A dragon," I said.

I almost didn't say it for fear of sounding silly, but the thought occurred, and, feeling as if I was in one of those dreams where you stand naked in front of a crowd, I spoke the words before I could get into my own way.

Lenny peered down at the pool for a long moment.

"Yes," she said, at last. "But not a normal dragon."

"No," I agreed. "This one is different."

So we invented a dragon, or discovered it, depending on your point of view. Our dragon was small and slender and lithe. It lived at the bottom of the pool, which was a nectar purer than water. It moved like the snake and flashed iridescent like the fish. It flew as it swam, but preferred water to air. It could converse directly with any mind—no need for tools as blunt as words. It could venture between worlds and across dimensions, but had never done so because it saw that all the tangled threads of reality could be woven and unraveled from this pool at the base of this tree on this ridge above this island in this lake.

It was curious and romantic and naive about things to which humans were jaded and jaded to things about which humans were naive. It was immortal not because it could not die, but because having encountered it, not even the most callous dragon slayer could bring them-selves to do it harm. It recognized no boundary between space and time. It ate ideas. The only treasure it hoarded was music. Though it had no voice, it loved to sing. When it opened its fanged mouth, it breathed no fire and made no sound, but sang rainbows. If you wished to meet it, you had to offer it a song, and, if you sang with true feeling, it would emerge from the depths and join the chorus, harmonizing great arcs of shattered light to the melody.

This was my first encounter with our dragon. Its name was not a word, but a feeling: the sense of willing vulnerability to whatever the future held in store, tinged with a bitter-sweet nostalgia for days long past.

23

"Let's make a deal," said Lenny.

"What kind of deal?" I asked, staring down into the dragon's pool.

"When we talk to each other like this," she said. "Just the two of us, we'll say what we mean."

She spat into her palm and reached around the trunk separating us.

After a brief hesitation, I reciprocated.

We shook, then wiped our hands on the rough bark.

24

Descending the gorge, I vibrated like a tuning fork. Water roared through the narrow chasm. Every step was treacherous, every hold slick with spray, our headlamps a feeble defense against the inky darkness, but none of it could touch me.

I always started the first day of school after summer break with a false sense of hope. Inevitably, some kids would have transferred to other schools, and strangers would have transferred in. Some kids had gone through growth spurts. Some had gone to science camp and some to soccer camp and some had holed up in the local library to avoid trouble at home. Some new friendships had formed, and some had fallen apart. Hearts had been broken and mended.

In this great reshuffling, it seemed possible that I could defy the odds and become cool. Someone entirely at home in their skin. Someone who knew what was really going on. Someone self-contained, self-aware, self-satisfied. Someone sought after. Someone who gave zero fucks, thereby earning the respect and admiration of their peers.

It only ever took a few days for this aspiration to sour. Cliques coalesced, and I wasn't among the chosen few. All it took was a snide comment, a sidelong glance, and I would discover, once again, that everyone had been busy playing an invisible game governed by opaque rules. It was already too late for me to even participate, let alone catch up. I gave too many fucks. So I'd tell myself I was above it all and retreat into *The Singularity Amulet* or *Quinten's Kernel*.

I wanted to be an insider, to feel like I was a member of an inner circle, and the more I wanted it, the more deftly it eluded me.

But this. *Let's make a deal.* Palm to saliva-lubricated palm. This was precisely the kind of conspiracy I had always dreamed of being party to.

Lenny was a person who did things. Who acted on her ideas. Who went after what she wanted. She generated momentum that pulled other people along in her wake. It was intoxicating. I wanted to be around her because life became more interesting around her, as if her presence was a black light illuminating marvelous illustrations that were otherwise invisible. A world with her in it was better than anything Clandestine Studios could dream up.

Tearing my eyes away from the search for the next foothold, I looked up at Lenny's retreating back.

She was gone.

25

My FLASHLIGHT BEAM found nothing but sheer granite walls and churning torrent.

Lenny was gone.

I was alone.

The roaring darkness surged around me. Our island camp suddenly felt like the other side of the galaxy. San Francisco may as well have been in a different universe.

Panic welled up inside me. My limbs refused to move. My thoughts raced in tight circles, going nowhere.

Then, above the water's thunder, a high-pitched sound: the yelp of an animal in pain.

26

Lenny lay at the base of the gorge, just a few feet from where we'd eaten our apples. A gash on her cheekbone wept blood. Her jacket was shredded. Her eyes were squeezed shut. My first terrified thought was that she was dead, but then her body shifted and another yelp escaped her, the sound sliding down into a raw moan.

Stumbling forward, I called out her name.

She shifted again. Yelped again.

Then I was at her side. I touched her shoulder to let her know I was there. Her flashlight was gone. I angled mine down so it wasn't in her face.

"I'm ok," she said, but her face was tight, and when she opened her eyes, her pupils were black beads in a sea of green. My stomach clenched.

"What about our deal?" I asked.

She blinked, then snorted a half-chuckle. "Ok," she said. "I'm fucked up. Happy?"

"Overjoyed," I said, trying to buoy both of us with irony as I looked up at the bus-sized boulder she had tumbled down. A scrap of Gore-Tex flapped from a protrusion of rock. I tasted blood, and realized I was chewing the inside of my lip.

"Can you stand?" I asked. "Here, let me help you up."

"Yeah, I think so," she said.

I slotted my right arm under her left armpit and supported her as she pushed herself up. She was shaky, but able. I suppressed a sigh of relief. We could make it back.

It was going to be ok.

Then she took a step, screamed, and collapsed as her right leg crumpled beneath her. I followed her to the ground, trying to break her fall. Moaning, she clutched at her right leg, waves of trembling pulsing through her body.

Guilt compounded my rising panic.

As delicately as I could, I pulled up the hem of her pants. Her foot rested at an unnatural angle. Something sharp jutted out from inside her sock around the ankle, stretching the once-colorful wool which was now stained dark and sticky.

"How bad is it?" she asked in a fragile voice between ragged breaths.

I opened my mouth to speak and vomited, managing to turn my head just in time to keep the puke off her. My throat burned and my head swam. I tasted apple and bile and fought against a sudden, overwhelming urge to faint.

"It's fine," I said, forcing a breath.

Her eyes narrowed.

"Ok, ok," I said. "You're fucked up. Happy?"

27

SAFELY HOLED UP in my bedroom, I loved playing games that put me into dangerous situations. I had robbed Fort Knox, made it out of the labyrinth ahead of the minotaur, survived an alternate dimension where a single misstep trapped you in an infinite memory loop, disarmed nuclear devices with seven seconds left in the countdown, and defeated Darth Vader in single combat.

This was not like that.

There was no way Lenny was going to make it back. There was no way I could leave her here while I went for help. There was no way we could stay where we were. There was no way anyone else would know we were here.

I wished I'd ignored Lenny's mysterious invitation. I wished I hadn't shown her my sketchbook. I wished she'd never found my secret rock. I wished my parents hadn't forced me to come on this trip.

If I hadn't opened up to her, we'd never have ended up here. Helpless. Stranded. No way to restart from a previous save point. This is what I got for putting myself out there, for believing I could be one of the cool kids, for throwing caution to the wind and taking real risks.

Someone needed to tell me what to do, to step in and fix things. I didn't ask for this. All I wanted was to be playing *Ark of the Shadow Moon.*

And then I looked over at Lenny and my burgeoning resentment at the injustice of it all melted in the face of her naked pain. This wasn't a game. Nobody was coming for us. I had felt the thrill of adventure as we snuck out of camp, and adventure had come to collect its due.

28

I TOOK OFF MY JACKET and wrapped it around Lenny's trembling body. She didn't object, which I took as a bad sign. Then I hooked my left arm under her right armpit and hoisted her up. She stood on her good leg, wavered, used my shoulders for support.

She hopped her good leg forward and I took her weight so her broken ankle didn't have to. We took a second step. A third. A fourth. By the twelfth step, we were both panting. By the thirtieth, I was soaked in sweat.

"I don't think I can do this," said Lenny.

"You can," I said. "We can."

Ten more steps.

"I can't," she stifled a sob. "It's so far."

She wasn't wrong. It was so, so far. Space and time had dilated, opening an abyss we had no hope of crossing. We needed to be anywhere but here, anytime but now. We needed a magic carpet, a teleportation device, an escape hatch.

"Remember our dragon?" I asked.

Two steps. *Not nothing*, I thought.

"Yes," she said, uncertain.

"Every dragon has a story," I said.

29

So I told Lenny the dragon's story.

Teeth chattering, I told her how it was born with the mountains it called home, how its fetus formed in the magma that solidified into the Sierra Nevada Batholith, how it was crushed, faulted, and uplifted as the Farallon Plate subducted under the North American plate, a creature of the Earth's core forced from the intense heat and pressure of its geological womb into the airy freedom of life on the surface. I told her about how Ice Age glaciers carved out valleys and sculpted ridge-lines, the jagged peaks of the young mountains that were its siblings matching the sharp edges of the dragon's adolescent personality, and how time eroded both into something like wisdom. I told her how the dragon was fascinated by the life that had grown up around it, from the grizzlies that used to roam these parts, to the humans who came to enjoy the lake, to the Clark's nutcracker that planted the whitebark pine that had been the object of our quest.

When I felt Lenny's energy flagging, I introduced a new complication. When her breathing got shallower, I would pay off some narrative element I had previously set up. When she shivered, I accelerated the pacing. When an involuntary moan escaped her, I inserted a plot twist.

I poured myself into the tale.

Nothing existed but the narrative.

30

THE STORY CARRIED US to the kayak, and as we struck out across the lake, Lenny huddled in the front, me paddling from the back, every muscle on fire, I began to sing.

I'm a terrible singer, and I don't know many songs, so I sang what I knew: Happy Birthday, Twinkle Twinkle Little Star, that kind of thing. After a few bars, Lenny's voice joined mine, weak, trembling, off-key, but present: proof of life.

And then there was a flash of movement in my peripheral vision and the dragon burst from the surface of the lake, shaking spray off its iridescent scales as its great wings scooped the frigid air. It spiraled around us in exquisitely graceful loops, the aerial acrobatics matching the song's rhythm. As we launched into the next verse, it joined in, although no sound escaped it. Instead, rainbows burst from its fanged jaws, drawing glowing arches across the dome of stars. Each strand of color rippled and throbbed with the music, the light dancing and bending and braiding itself into complex, constantly shifting patterns that vibrated against the infinite dark.

I had never seen anything like it before. I have never seen anything like it since. You might say we were in shock. You might say we were projecting. You might say we were feverish and exhausted and out of our depth and out of our minds. And you'd be right.

But Lenny and I knew what we saw that night, and we've never felt the need to justify it, because we've never shared it with anyone, until you, now.

31

Everything after that sort of blends together in my memory, though a few moments stand out.

The adults standing on the rocky beach as we arrived back at the island, desperate with worry. They had realized we were missing and spent the preceding hour scouring any hiding places they could think of before hearing our singing echo across the lake.

After the immediate provision of first aid to Lenny's injuries, finding ourselves at the center of a group huddle that focused collective emotion like a magnifying glass does sunlight. Me, the shy loner, shocking everyone by proactively claiming that the whole thing had been my idea, my not-quite-lie derailing the blame that would have otherwise fallen on Lenny's shoulders, notorious troublemaker that she was.

The mad rush to pack up camp and get Lenny to a hospital. Working with Theo to load gear into the cars and the effortless grace with which he accepted my apology for being such a jerk to him. (Years later, when I asked Theo to be the best man at our wedding, I would look back on that moment as a shining example of how he lives by giving everyone and everything the benefit of the doubt and, as a result, sees nothing but beauty.)

The ER doc with a penchant for gallows humor reassuring the anxious group that Lenny's injuries were serious, but not life-threatening. She had a badly broken ankle, two broken ribs, a sprained wrist, and a concussion, in addition to superficial scrapes and bruises.

My parents interrogating me on the long ride home until I explained that I knew their stunt with the hairpin turn had been a contrived way to get me to emotionally invest in a trip I hadn't consented to, and that if they wanted to force me to get outside, they should expect unforeseen consequences. Also, I told them I had had a lot of fun despite myself because nothing sabotages a guilt trip like telling someone they were right all along. It was true: I had learned that you could become so bewitched by a seductive *elsewhere* that you missed out on ever being truly *here*, and yet, elsewhere was sometimes exactly where you needed to go.

The sun setting beyond the Golden Gate as we crossed the Bay Bridge, the dying light submerging San Francisco in amber, towers glowing, textures popping. It was home, but the sense of comfort the familiar skyline normally evoked was laced with a strange intimation of novelty, as if something had shifted in our absence. This was a city brimming with secrets and dreams and drama. A place that was always in the process of becoming something new.

A place where anyone could reinvent themselves.

32

WHEN I GOT HOME, I did not play *Ark of the Shadow Moon.*

It wasn't that it had lost its appeal, but that a greater impulse had eclipsed it. Just as the games I loved so much had beamed me from my cluttered bedroom to the outer reaches of the galaxy, so the dragon's story had transported Lenny from pain's ratcheting vice to another plane, a reprieve that enabled our safe escape. This was true magic. Games, books, movies, music, art—all drew their power from the stories they told. Stories were teleportation devices, and as much as I enjoyed being teleported, more than anything I wanted to offer that gift to others, to enchant them as I had Lenny.

So I opened my sketchbook and began designing a game of my own, a game that would invite players into a new kind of conversation with reality, a game that honored everything I loved about games, a game that offered a means of escape that was not a cheap trick or a mere diversion but a place from which to gain a new vantage on yourself, because the only way out of an untenable situation is to become a person that can handle that situation.

When I released it seven months later, my first game was weird in the startling way that only an autodidact adolescent's uncompromising solo project can be weird. But the weirdest part was how many players it attracted, and how hard they fell in love with it. Some people hated it, of course. And most people just didn't get it. But those that did could find no substitute for the singular experience, and their gratitude catapulted me into making my next game, and, ultimately, making a life of making games.

33

So, how do you make a game?

The same way you make any other worthy contribution to this strange and beautiful world we are fortunate enough to share, however briefly. You put yourself on the hook. You fill the gap in the universe only you can see. You use your gifts to make gifts for people you care about.

For me, all of it, every last bit, is about tapping into how it felt to show Lenny my drawings of that whitebark pine all those decades ago, to tell her a story as we stumbled, broken, down that mountain. How I could make something that could move someone, and how that someone moved me, and continues to move me a lifetime later, even as I sit here by her bedside, writing this sentence while listening to the gentle ebb and flow of her shallow breathing, waiting, grateful and heartbroken, for your grandmother to embark on her next great adventure, the one that awaits us all.

The End

Writing *Ensorcelled*

WHEN MY SON was born, I became hyper-aware of how often I checked my phone. For me, the screen was a window into the manifold wonders of the internet. For him, I was staring at a boring metallic rectangle instead of the manifold wonders of the world he'd just arrived in.

So I set my phone aside and made a habit of not using it in his presence. Another habit I developed was inventing bedtime stories for him every night. I may have written twelve novels, but I can tell you that improvising full narrative arcs that fit into five minutes was surprisingly challenging.

One of those stories gave me the idea for *Ensorcelled*, and I started writing it when I wasn't changing diapers. As I wrote, a strange realization slowly dawned on me.

I had set my phone aside because it teleported me out of the here and now and into a feed, a text, a meme, a video, an essay. It captured my attention. It compelled me to scroll. But wasn't that precisely what I was seeking to do when I told my son a bedtime story? To capture his attention. To transport him *elsewhere*. To make him want to find out what happened next.

There are ancient myths about shape-shifters who can turn themselves into grizzlies, seals, and falcons. But if they're not careful, those who take animal form can become so immersed in the supernatural experience that they lose their human selves forever.

Art enchants us. Technology can too. Taking you beyond yourself is beautiful and danger-ous. The trick is remembering to come back, having gained a new perspective.

If you're reading this sentence, *Ensorcelled* enchanted you, and if you enjoyed it, please help bring the magic to others by recommending it to friends and posting reviews. Books thrive on word of mouth, especially odd little books like this one that don't have massive marketing engines behind them like *Ark of the Shadow Moon.*

Thanks

To Brad Feld and Amy Bachelor for supporting *Ensorcelled* with a generous grant.

To Peter Nowell for designing the book, inside and out.

To Josh Anon for giving invaluable notes on early drafts.

To Pamela Lorence for directing and producing the audiobook.

To Craig Mod for unknowingly providing the perfect title during an unrelated interview.

To Sierra and Dave for organizing the camping trips that inspired Tam's.

To my newsletter subscribers for their undying support and enthusiasm.

To Drea, Ash, and Claire for being who they are. I love you more each and every day.

And to you, dear reader, for allowing yourself to be ensorcelled by *Ensorcelled*—may you find your dragon, and someone to share it with.

About the Author

Eliot Peper is the bestselling author of twelve novels, including *Bandwidth*, *Cumulus*, and *Foundry*. He also helps build technology businesses and is the head of story at Portola, where he leads lore and narrative engineering. The best way to follow his writing is to subscribe to his newsletter.

eliotpeper.com